D1370388

MAX and RUBY

in Pandora's Box

MAX and RUBY

in Pandora's Box

Rosemary Wells

PUFFIN BOOKS

• *For the Vrachnos family* •

PUFFIN BOOKS
Published by the Penguin Group
Penguin Putnam Inc., 375 Hudson Street, New York, New York 10014, U.S.A.
Penguin Books Ltd, 27 Wrights Lane, London W8 5TZ, England
Penguin Books Australia Ltd, Ringwood, Victoria, Australia
Penguin Books Canada Ltd, 10 Alcorn Avenue, Toronto, Ontario, Canada M4V 3B2
Penguin Books (N.Z.) Ltd, 182-190 Wairau Road, Auckland 10, New Zealand

Penguin Books Ltd, Registered Offices: Harmondsworth, Middlesex, England

First published in the United States by Dial Books for Young Readers, a division of Penguin Books USA Inc., 1993
Originally published under the title *Max and Ruby's First Greek Myth: Pandora's Box*
Published by Puffin Books, a member of Penguin Putnam Books for Young Readers, 1998

11

THE LIBRARY OF CONGRESS HAS CATALOGED THE DIAL EDITION AS FOLLOWS:
Wells, Rosemary.
Max and Ruby's first Greek myth Pandora's Box / Rosemary Wells.
Summary / Ruby tries to stop her younger brother Max from sneaking into her room and
snooping by reading him an altered version of "Pandora's Box."
ISBN 0-8037-1524-2.—ISBN 0-8037-1525-0 (lib. bdg.)
[1. Brothers and sisters—Fiction. 2. Curiosity—Fiction. 3. Rabbits—Fiction.]
I. Title.
PZ7.W46843Pan 1993 [E]—dc20 92-30332 CIP AC

Puffin Books ISBN 0-14-056415-2

Manufactured in China
Typography by Jane Byers Bierhorst

The artwork for each picture is an ink drawing with watercolor painting.

Max's sister Ruby put a sign on the door of her room.
"This means you, Max," said Ruby.
"Can you read it?"
"Yes," said Max.

But Max had no idea what the sign said.

When Ruby wasn't looking, he sneaked into her room
to see what was in her jewelry box.

Ruby caught him.

"Max," said Ruby, "can't you read what this sign says?"
"No!" said Max.
   Ruby read him the sign out loud three times.

Ruby made Max sit in her chair.
"Max, I'm going to read you a story about
sneaking and peeking.
Are you ready, Max?" asked Ruby.
"Yes," said Max.
"Then listen up," said Ruby.

Once upon a time there was a little girl named Pandora.
Pandora's mother had to go out to the store.
"Pandora," she said, "you may have a nice piece of
honey cake, and you may play in the sprinkler...

but you must promise not to open my magic jewelry box."
Pandora promised.

Pandora ate a delicious piece of honey cake,
and she played in the sprinkler, but she couldn't
keep her mind off that box.

Pandora tried to x-ray the box with her eyes.
"I think I see sugar lumps in there," she said.

Then she shook it. "I hear diamond rings," she said.

Pandora sat outside on the terraceum, away from
temptation, but a magnetic force propelled her inside.

So she just peeked in the box for half a second.

Out flew a hundred twister bees, a slew of fire ants,
and clouds of Mexican jumping weevils.

"Oh no! What will I do? What will Mother say?"
moaned Pandora.
Then through the huzz, buzz, and fluttering of
a thousand tiny wings, she heard a muffled
voice cry, "Let me out!"

Left inside the forbidden box was a little green spider.
"Eek!" yelled Pandora.
"I'm your only hope!" said the spider. "Slam that
lid on me and you're a dead duck!"

The spider spun a web so big, wide, and wonderful
that she caught every twister bee, fire ant, and
Mexican jumping weevil in sight.
Then she ate them all.

"I am going back to bed, Pandora," said the spider,
"but you must promise that you will never snoop again."
"Never, never again!" promised Pandora.

When Pandora's mother returned, the house
was entirely bug-free.
"What a good bunny you are!" said her mother.
"I'm going to take you out to the movies!"

"You can wear my gold necklace…

and I'll wear my emerald pin," said Pandora's mother.

Ruby closed the book.

"What did Pandora's sign say, Max?" asked Ruby.

"No!" said Max.

"And what does my sign say, Max?" asked Ruby.

"No!" said Max.

"And who does it mean, Max?" Ruby asked.

"You!" said Max.